For YOU

This book is on Zahra.

It was December when Zahra's mother went from the UK to Pakistan and died there.

Zahra then went from one mosque to another; she also did her best surveying work in UK Local Government as Director.

Zahra became a Chartered Surveyor and a Fellow of the Royal Institution of Chartered Surveyors.

Zahra already had an MBA in Construction and Real Estate and a twenty-year career in affordable housebuilding.

Zahra is not a religious scholar, but she has read about faith a lot.

This is Zahra's story of three generations; it is her story of pilgrimage and life journey; she shares her story as it may help someone.

Zahra learned a lot since her mother went ten years ago.

This book is for YOU.

About the Author

The Author has a similar journey as Zahra.

Sarah is a British-born Muslim Woman with Pakistani Heritage.

Sarah has an MBA in Construction and Real Estate; she is a Chartered Surveyor and a Fellow of the Royal Institution of Chartered Surveyors.

Sarah is one of the First South Asian Women with a 30-year career in Corporate Real Estate in the UK; she worked in both UK Local Government as Director and in Housing as Board Member, as well as in the Charity Sector.

Sarah is also one of the first Muslim Women to do Hajj alone in 2022.

Sarah has put much personal effort into this book, this is her first book, and she hopes you enjoy it.

From, Sarah Manzoor, MBA FRICS

Intention

Zahra has read that every person of faith must read about what they follow and understand according to their capacity.

If someone attains knowledge or understanding through study, contemplation, and the test of life, they must teach others and share the joy and peace from contact with the spiritual world.

Each book on faith must be read with the tongue, voice, and eyes and with the best light, our intellect can supply.

Even more with the most natural light, which our heart and conscience can give us, I write with this spirit.

Zahra writes as through faith, she found freedom.

Zahra

Thank you

This is a Fictional book, the places may be real, but they are not. Also, the characters are made up or may as well be. Thank you to anyone that has been part of Zahra's journey so far …

Contents

The Opening

In the name of God (Allah), All beneficent, All-merciful

Introduction

In 2019 Zahra first tried to do Hajj. Hajj is the fifth pillar of Islam. It is the pilgrimage to Makkah in Saudi Arabia.

Then the Covid pandemic hit, and everything went into lockdown. Zahra began to walk in nature. Many people entered this bizarre virtual world.

In 2020 she began to read the Quran with meaning. A year ago, she stopped working too. Zahra has no parents or husband; her sisters are busy, and her sons are too.

In 2022 Zahra was to turn fifty. With less to do, she wondered what to do next.

Then in 2022, Allah invited Zahra to do Hajj. Then she began to reflect on life. This is Zahra's reflection on life. With a little on her Hajj journey.

Zahra is the Pilgrim.
The (Jobless) Lonely Old Woman.

Chapter 1. Context

Picture a blue sky and white clouds; it is a warm day. There are trees, a hill, and a field in the countryside; it looks beautiful. It is St. Albans, in the United Kingdom. This was Belinda's photo from October 2020. Zahra likes Belinda's photos a lot.

At One with Nature

Also, picture a beautiful red-leaved tree. It is the morning, about sunrise. The sun shines through the red tree. Below the tree is a lake; the sun shines through to the tree, to the water, and reflects. Around the lake are more trees. It is a lovely autumn day.

The picture is from Ravenscourt Park in Hammersmith, West London, UK. Zahra took the photo in October 2020.

In 2019 Zahra began to walk 5km each day.

In 2020 She entered a footstep competition at work. Belinda, Zahra's footstep friend, and Zahra did 30,000+ steps daily; they did 1,328,203 in 21 days and three weeks. They won the worldwide competition.

They had two other people on their team; they did not do much, two men. But one man supported both Belinda and Zahra a lot.

As Zahra walked, she marvelled at Allah's creation. Anything Zahra finds beautiful; she takes photos off. Her phone is full of pictures of nature. Belinda would send Zahra photos too on WhatsApp. Zahra was drawn to nature. Zahra was out first thing when everyone would sleep, Belinda in another place.

Allah says the creation of the Earth and Heavens are signs for people of understanding, Quran 3:190. As Zahra went out daily for many months, she tuned in with nature. Then in 2022, Zahra walked the London marathon, all 26.2 miles; she did that in 2021 too.

The Muslim Religious Scholar

"Sufficient for us is Allah, and (He is) the best Disposer of affairs" Quran 3:173.

This is Nadeer's WhatsApp status update for December 2020; it is read for distress; he posted a photo with both Quranic Arabic and Urdu text. Zahra was annoyed at Nadeer as she did not like that, he commented on a woman in her profile picture.

In 2020 Zahra made a WhatsApp friend called Nadeer. They started to talk during Ramadan as they liked similar things. Nadeer's real name is a friend.

Nadeer used to post many religious things. In private, he used to tell Zahra silly things. She used to say to Nadeer, "you make things up. Please tell me who you are." Nadeer did not tell Zahra, so she told him, and he blocked her.

Then Zahra connected with a lot of UK Sufi Groups to find him. Zahra also began to read about Islam, listen to stories on the life of the Prophet Muhammad, and read his sayings.

In Ramadan 2021, Nadeer came back. One day she went to see him with Eid gifts. He said, "no one would come from London to Manchester with gifts." Zahra said, "I do." Nadeer was being silly, and since they are friends. Nadeer's past behaviour reminded Zahra of a book.

The book was called "The Kite Runner" by Khaled Hossein. It was published in 2003. It is set in Kabul in, Afghanistan. It tells a story of a young boy subjected to inappropriate adult behaviour; in British Muslim cultures, people are told: "not to speak."

Nadeer taught Zahra that not all religious people are always good and to be careful. Zahra's English friends say, "such people can be from other religions too." In 2022 Zahra talked to many people and questioned how there could be so many victims.

It is why Zahra used to avoid such people in the past. But Nadeer is not a Muslim Religious Scholar. He is a lawyer that specialises in divorce. He named Zahra, Zahra. Zahra has the same name as the Prophet Muhammad's daughter, Fatimah Zahra; he loved her.

Allah Made You OK

The Quds Wall can be found in the West London Islamic Centre, West Ealing, London, UK. Zahra associates the Centre with Salman. The Centre is a £7.5m new mosque; it is very beautiful.

The Quds Wall has yellow and blue tiles. A yellow tile costs £5,000, the blue £1,500 and your name is engraved on the wall. The donation goes towards construction costs.

Zahra has a brother. His name is Salman. Salman tells Zahra she is "awkward, difficult, and obstructive." He tells Zahra ", You cannot help that Allah gave you intelligence." Salman's real name is star.

Zahra told Salman she snuck into one of his events. Salman said, "do not worry, I am your brother; I paid." While Zahra said, "I have no brother."

Over the Covid pandemic, Zahra has accepted Salman as her brother. They began to talk on WhatsApp about Islam often.

What Zahra liked about Salman most is that while Salman is a big businessperson. He appreciates his family and the people with him. All the people associated with Salman have been good men.

At one stage, Zahra only worked and cared for her children; she did everything but did not think she was enough. Salman taught Zahra, "She is OK," and if someone likes her, they will.

Salman made Zahra see that not all people are the same. Zahra then began to allow new people into her life.

Salman also told Zahra how to beat Belinda, which she did once.

He also said, "to go direct to Allah," which she did. Before, she used to follow many people, but when they turned away from her, she was forced to go direct to Allah. Slowly she began to discover she preferred it like that.

When Salman once turned up at Zahra's home, she said a few years later, "why did you come? I did not like that." Salman said, "look, I freed you from all that." Zahra said, "OK," she was unsure.

As Salman is who he is and Zahra has high regard for him, learning to accept herself through him and others freed her.

When the Black convert Bilal became Muslim, his masters tortured him; he would not renounce Islam. Prophet Muhammad sent his friend Abu Bakr to free him, and Salman and Zahra's story was similar.

Zahra was caught up in many old cultural things and reading about Islam has taught her to let many old things go.

Salman said, "Allah feeds his birds," and in 2022, Zahra took a break from work.

After 34 years of work, Zahra is jobless.

A New Muslim

Picture a path with trees on either side. Ahead is a lake and the morning sun. The weather is nice. The picture was taken in Kensington Gardens, London, UK. Zahra took the photo in October 2020 at sunrise.

In 2020 Zahra began to listen to Shaykh Yasir Qadhi's lectures. Shaykh's 103 one-hour lectures are on the Seerah of the Prophet Muhammad. They are on Islamic History and the Life of the Prophet Muhammad.

In Ramadan 2021 Zahra's elder Sufi sister Rahma. Rahma's real name means to Protect. Rehma posted a thinking point from the Quran. Rahma posted on her WhatsApp status.

As the text was in English, Zahra asked what Rahma had read. Rahma said she read the Majestic Quran by Musharraf Hussain.

Zahra ordered a copy; the text says, "The opening of the heart and mind to divine message is a special favour from Allah." In the Majestic Quran by Musharraf Hussain, the words are very deep.

In 2019 and 2020, also 2021 too, UK mosques were closed. During Ramadan, Zahra read Taraweeh at home. Taraweeh is extra nights prayers one reads during Ramadan. When one reads Taraweeh, one reads the Quran.

In 2019 and 2020, Zahra read the Quran in Quranic Arabic; in 2021, she read in English too. As the Quran's helped Zahra, she offered to buy some for others.

In 2022, Zahra went to Central London Mosque to record the Iman's recitation of the Quran. An Imam is someone that leads congregational prayers. Zahra would then listen and try to find the text in the Quran.

If Zahra could not find the text, she would ask her Hafiz friend. A Hafiz is someone that has memorised all the Quran.

Slowly each chapter and verse of the Quran took on a new meaning for Zahra. Zahra's Quranic Arabic is still not strong, but she is tuned in. For Zahra to read the Quran with meaning gave Islam a whole new meaning.

Zahra found care, choice, compassion, and kindness; she learned that humans are not perfect, so do your best. Allah says there is no compulsion in religion, Quran 2:256. The verse comes after the Throne Verse called Ayat al Kursi and is a reminder that people can choose a path.

Zahra does not know why she finds it all so interesting, but she did and does still, although she does struggle too.

A Journey of a Lifetime

Hajj, A Journey of a Lifetime by Fisabilillah Publications, is a book. Zahra was given the book in 2016 when she went to Umrah.

The front of the book tells pilgrims how to perform Umrah, and the rest is on Hajj. The books were particularly good; they were free.

Umrah is a little Muslim pilgrimage.

The Hajj is the annual pilgrimage to Makkah. It means "to intend a journey." Muslims are expected to do Hajj once in their life if they can. People can then call themselves Haji or Hajjan.

The Hajj is the fifth pillar of Islam.

The other four pillars are:

Shahadah is the declaration of faith.

Salah is the five daily prayers.

Zakat, which is a charity.

Sawn, which is too fast in the month of Ramadan.

Hajj takes place in Dhu al-Hijrah, the last month in the Islamic calendar.

The Islamic calendar is different from the Gregorian calendar. The Islamic calendar started when the Prophet Muhammad migrated to Madinah.

In 2022 Hajj was in July.

One in a Million

"British Hajj pilgrim says she feels 'very blessed' to be one in a million," Arab News on 29 June 2022.

The article featured a photo from Masjid Al-Haram, the new section, from December 2016.

The picture is of Zahra and her son, they were the only people in the new area then, and her younger son took the photo. Allah; always made Zahra and her sons very welcome. He even gave them their own private space in His house.

Arab News used Zahra's image from 2016 in the article in June 2022.

Zahra wanted to do Hajj in 2019. Zahra did not go as she had no one to go with. Then for two years, no international pilgrims were allowed. Covid has made it difficult to travel.

Then in 2021, after 1,400 years, rulings changed. Women can now do Hajj alone; this created an opportunity for Zahra.

In 2022 it was announced that one million pilgrims would be permitted.

Dome Tours, a UK tour operator, offered Zahra a place and she paid as soon as possible to reserve her space; it was very emotional to book to go alone.

Then Dome Tours said the system had changed. Zahra then entered a draw for one of the one million places. Zahra was selected.

It took much work to book on a system run by Motawif. But Zahra did book Hajj. Zahra just wanted to go in the end, and she did not care what star rating and where she stayed; all she knew what that she wanted to go.

Zahra also got all her money back from Dome Tours; it was nice that they prioritised their sister's money.

Muslims believe the names of Pilgrims are decided during Ramadan. They say it is on the night of decree. A decree means an official order. The night of decree is in the last ten nights of Ramadan, the odd nights.

Allah had invited Zahra; she was lucky, and the Arab News article captured Zahra's thoughts very well.

Chapter 2. Childhood

In December 2016, it was sunset. Zahra was with her two sons.

Zahra took a photo of a path leading to the sea; it was taken on a beach. Ahead is the open sky; it had black and orange clouds. It is a warm evening.

The photo was taken at the Lowest Point on Earth, the Dead Sea in Jordan.

As well as Zahra's two sons, the lonely old Muslim woman was with her too.

The view was stunning. In some way, this was the start of Zahra's Hajj journey; she did not know then.

The Lonely Old Muslim Woman

Zahra took another photo in December 2016. Zahra was there with her two sons.

The picture is of the inside of a mosque. The carpet is red and gold. It is an old mosque. Ahead is a chandelier with the lights on. There are few people. The photo is of Masjid Al Aqsa next to the Dome of the Rock, Israel.

The Al Aqsa Masjid is a proper old mosque; when you go for morning prayers, there are no lights, and you can hardly see anything when you walk to the mosque in the morning. Then after morning prayers, it is lovely to see the morning light.

As you walk to the mosque, you can hear the imam reading text from the Quran.

Zahra also liked that there was no separation between men and women. Women came in from the back, and the ones that came first sat on the line right at the back. Men that came in first sat on the line at the front. Then as the masjid filled up, the lines in the middle filled up too.

From the masjid, Zahra learned there is no harm in women being at the back as that has dignity. Zahra likes that, although she is "old school" and traditional in thought.

Zahra was sad she was to go Hajj alone, and she cried a lot, but from the first day Nadeer saw Zahra's face, he said, "you cry a lot."

Zahra remembers. On Christmas Day in 2016, she arrived at the lowest point on earth, the Dead Sea in Jordan. This was after her trip to Al Aqsa Mosque in Israel. Zahra was with her two sons. Zahra and her sons were to travel to Makkah next for Umrah.

They were only to stay in Jordan for one night. As it was Maghreb evening prayer time, Zahra did not want to miss the sunset. Zahra said to her sons, "as soon as we stop, let us go to the sea."

As they walked to the sea, this old lady in all black followed them. At sea, she pulled her dress up and went in.

The old lady later said to Zahra that she "travels alone." The old lady said she "has a family." She said she finds it "very difficult with them." The lady said, "she is happy alone." Zahra, with her two sons, thought it was sad.

Zahra did not imagine that five years later, she would do Hajj alone. After lockdowns, Zahra decided one ought to take the opportunity. Then in 2022, when this other old lady said it was not right that Zahra went alone, she was right. Hajj made Zahra reflect on life a lot.

Zahra was now the lonely old Muslim Woman too; she was no longer a little girl.

Passport to Heaven

Zahra has a photo of a person holding a child; this is Zahra's dad and Zahra; the photo might be from about 1974. Zahra looks like she may be 18 months or two years of age.

Zahra's dad wears a white shirt, a black tie, and yellow braces. He has black trousers on. He is a slim man; he is smart. Zahra is wearing a red sleeveless dress; she has white shoes on; they look like soft trainers. Zahra is a medium-sized child, not too big or too small.

The photo was taken in Weston Super Mare, Avon, UK. Both Zahra and her dad have the same deep-set eyes.

Zahra was born on 14 August 1972. 14 August is Pakistan Day. India Pakistan partition took place in 1947.

Zahra's parents were born in what would have been India then. Zahra's parents later say they were from Pakistan. Zahra's parents were Muslim.

Zahra was born in the United Kingdom.

Zahra is a girl.

Zahra had two sisters, one born in 1967 and one in 1973.

Due to the old Pakistani mentality. People said Zahra's father "did not want daughters." When Zahra asked her father before he died, he said, "that was not true." He said, "I am very happy I have all three of you."

Zahra thought that she had to be the son when she grew up. People later said Zahra was her "mother's son."

Zahra's cousins say Zahra's dad "was proud of her." The Prophet Muhammad said, "daughters are your passport to heaven. Provided you take care of them." In 2022, India, Pakistan, and China have the highest rate of sex-selective abortions, which is sad.

Zahra's cousins say Zahra's dad told them stories of her and her work; even though she only worked in Safeway (the supermarket) when he was around, he told them the store manager would tell Zahra's dad how hard she worked.

Safeway's promoted Zahra three times in 2 years; when she left, she ran a department; they said, "Zahra was very good at customer service," and they gave her an award too.

Then Zahra worked in Housing and Real Estate.

Zahra is a British-born Muslim with a Pakistani heritage.

Home

Zahra's photo for this page was many rose petals on her dad's grave.

Zahra's fathers made them lots of homes. Zahra was born in her father's friend's house in Weston Super Mare, Avon.

Zahra's family home was in Shepherds Bush, West London.

Zahra's father and brother built their mother a home in Sialkot, Pakistan.

Zahra's father built his family home in Sialkot in, Pakistan.

Zahra's mother's father built his home in Gujranwala in Pakistan.

Zahra's mother's grandfather's home was in Jhelum in, Pakistan.

Zahra's father grew up in Wazirabad in, Pakistan.

In Wazirabad, the uncle Zahra's father grew up with, his home is in Lahore, Pakistan.

The family used to go to Pakistan every two years.

Then there were other homes in Mitranwali, Karachi, Lahore, and Islamabad.

After Zahra got married, she moved around. She found it hard to afford where the family lived. For a long time, she travelled one hundred miles for evening childcare.

Zahra's father's made homes, not properties, for a monopoly board game.

In 2022 Zahra's father's final home is his grave in Southall, Middlesex, UK, even though he was absent from the family in UK most of his later life.

In 2022 Zahra's mother's home is her grave in Jhelum, Pakistan, even though she was with the family in UK most of her later life.

Zahra lives in the UK.

Honour Your Father

Zahra put a photo into Word; the auto text tried to describe the photo. It said, "a picture of a street and a dirty basement," but this is the street view of the family home in Sialkot, Pakistan.

Zahra thinks the auto text does not like the street, but it was OK when Zahra was there for six months in 1986 during her GCSE. Zahra took the photo in March 2022.

Zahra's father was called Fakher. He was born in 1926. In 1926 he would have been born under the British Raj. Pakistan would have been India then. Fakher's parents were poor. After Fakher Iftikhar was ten years younger, there were five other brothers and one sister.

When Fakher was a child, he was sent to Wazirabad to grow up in a wealthy relatives' home. He became friends with the family's eldest son, who now lives in Lahore.

When Fakher returned to his mother, he was a man. In 1945 the Second World war ended. In 1947 the Indo-Pak partition took place. Fakher would have been 21 years of age.

The UK needed labour to rebuild after the war. Despite racism, many people like Fakher ended up in the UK. Fakher established himself.

In about 1965, when Fakher married, he had a restaurant and other property interests. His wife Khushi was twenty years younger than him.

First, they lived in Fakher's friend Mr. Hick's home, then they moved to London, and he came too. In London, they became part of the local community in Shepherds Bush. The family had a good life.

Fakher was respected; he fully financially provided for his family and supported his mother.

But he hit his wife, and in 1986 the family unit broke down. First, Fakher's elder daughter left; she was nineteen, and she got married. Then after taking the family to Pakistan, he went too.

Then he lived in Pakistan, and his family was eventually sent back to the UK.

Fakher died in 2004 in Ealing, London, UK. Fakher had lung cancer. He used to be a smoker; her father always struggled with ill health; the elders said, "he had a terrible roadside incident before he got married, and it took a long time for him to get better." He was addicted to sleeping pills once.

Fakher fully financially provided; he provided more than any man. He was a good man. But Allah say's do not hit your wife, Quran 4:34. In 2022, Pakistani and South Asians, Irish and white people, and others, including Black people, say domestic incidents in the older generation were common.

Fakher would have had a hard life, and it is sad how things turned out because, in 1993, he said, "wherever I am, and whatever I am doing, all my thoughts are always with all three of you."

In the same 1993 letter, he wrote about his happy memories of being one home; he said, "our problem is that we listen to others but not each other."

Zahra's father was right; other people's involvement is not good. Zahra's dad told her to "be brave."

Your Mother First

Zahra has a picture of a train track in Jhelum in Pakistan. Zahra took the photo in March 2022 after she visited her mother's grave. It is night-time and it is dark. As Zahra had never travelled on the train in Pakistan, her dad's brother was worried.

Fakher asked to see Khushi before he died, and she said "no."

Khushi grew up in Pakistan Jhelum. Khushi grew up in her grandfather's home with four brothers, a sister, and many uncles and aunts. One brother drowned at River Jhelum; she said, "they went on a picnic." Khushi's grandfather had a big house.

Khushi said, "she did not like school that much but did not particularly like English." From what she said, she had a happy childhood.

Khushi would have come to the UK in about 1965. Khushi said she was "not experienced in looking after children." She said, "the children were sick," well, Zahra and "her husband." She said, "different cultures, homesickness," that she says "bored, loneliness, and health problems."

She talks about "racism, discrimination, and prejudice." She says, "the police, verbal abuse (bad words), and physical attacks."

Khushi wrote those words in 1993. When Zahra read the words in 2022, she read that she was attacked in and outside the home. Khushi said, "she tried to be strong."

As a child, when unwell, Zahra hid under her bed so her dad would not get mad at her mum. Zahra sleepwalked; she dreamt of ghosts and snakes. Each daughter did what they could to stop the abuse and protect their mum.

Khushi was divorced around 1988. She then took care of her daughters and grandchildren. She relied on others for English. She liked to spend time with her friends. She lost her health early.

Khushi was diabetic, partially blind, and died when she was sixty-six. Khushi died in 2012 in Jhelum, Pakistan; they say, "she had a cardiac arrest," and she would have been born in 1946. She went to Pakistan for a six-week holiday and died the day before her scheduled flight back to London.

When the daughters tried to bring her back to London, she came to Zahra to say, "do not take me to London again," Zahra could feel she was saying "no."

While all the paperwork was done, and they had even bought a coffin to transport her, on the day her body was to be embalmed, Zahra said, "no," it made everyone mad, but Zahra said, "no."

In the end, all three sisters buried their mother in Pakistan as she wanted. It was a tough time for everyone, and very emotional.

Zahra's aunts say that before she went to Pakistan, she said to them, "Zahra is misunderstood; look after her." They said it was as if she knew she was going to Pakistan to die.

The daughters fought for fundamental human rights; they put their mother first. The Prophet Muhammad said your mother first three times and then your father. In 2022 Zahra found Khushi's note; the words are hers.

Zahra's mother said, "it is a man's role to provide for his family," until the day Khushi died, Zahra's father provided for his ex-wife, and from what he provided, she also helped her family.

Zahra's mother was right; men should provide for their families as Fakher did.

The Old Christian Man

Zahra has a photo of her dad and Mr. Hicks (Zahra's granddad). The image is outside Mr. Hicks's home in Weston Super Mare, Avon, UK. The image may be from 1965.

Mr. Hicks is wearing a black suit, trousers, and a jacket, as well as a black tie. He is smiling, a few inches taller than Zahra's dad, and smart. Zahra's father is wearing black trousers, a black tie, and a white shirt; he has a cardigan on top.

Behind them is a conservatory; Zahra assumes the photo was taken in the back garden of Mr. Hicks's home; it was a nice home where they all lived.

Mr. Hicks used to walk Zahra to primary school, Miles Coverdale in Shepherds Bush. Khushi and Jasmin Zahra's little sister were always late.

Mr. Hick was a British white Christian older man. He was Fakher's friend from Weston Super Mare. Mr. Hicks was always smartly dressed; he wore a shirt and tie, trousers, and a jacket. Zahra never saw him in casual wear or his pyjamas during the day.

Mr. Hicks had a set routine. He woke at 7.30 AM, had lunch at 1 PM and 2 PM, went for a walk, had 5 PM tea, 7 PM dinner, and eleven to bed. Mr. Hicks was mild-mannered; he did not swear or drink alcohol. He went to Church on Sunday; he celebrated Christmas and Easter, and Zahra did too. He did not work; he lived off property income.

In 1992 Mr. Hicks was diagnosed with Multiple Sclerosis.

He died in a home in Wales in 1994. He left his estate to his one cousin, Khushi, and all of Fakher's three daughters.

Mr. Hicks was the best man Zahra had ever met. He was caring, kind, and considerate and loved Zahra and her sisters. Mr. Hicks was safe and stable; he was the family's silent protector. Zahra never experienced racism growing up, as Mr. Hicks walked her to school.

Zahra had more problems with her people; Mr. Hicks protected her. He reminds Zahra of the Prophet Muhammad's uncle Abu

Talib. People say Abu Talib did not become Muslim, but he was the Protector of the Prophet Muhammad.

When Mr. Hicks died, some people said he should have become Muslim, but Zahra did not like that. When Abu Talib died, Allah told Prophet Muhammed not to ask similar, as it was between Allah and Abu Talib. Mr. Hicks was a good Christian man, and Zahra loved him.

Good people can come in all forms.

Chapter 3. Adulthood

A little girl in a green dress is running ahead of her mum and little sister.

Zahra's photo shows a medium-sized lady at the back, Zahra's mum was like that. She had a little girl on her right-hand side; she was holding her hand. The little girl has the same green dress as Zahra at the front.

Zahra's mum and Mubarak, her big sister, always made Zahra and her little sister Jasmin the same clothes. The green dresses are like ballet dancer dresses.

The picture is of a street, with shops on one side and a few more people in the dark at the back.

Zahra took the photo at Notting Hill Gate, London, UK, in 2021. It reminded Zahra of her mum and little sister; Zahra always went ahead as they were always late.

The little girl running ahead looks like she is still at primary school, but soon after that age, Zahra's father left his permanent place in their lives; Zahra was fourteen then.

First School

Zahra has a photo of someone sitting on a climbing frame of a teenager. That is Zahra's photo she took in Ravenscourt Park in Hammersmith, West London.

When Fakher left, Zahra used to suffer from bad asthma, she could not climb like that, but later she did. Zahra sat on top of a very high climbing frame with her torn white Nike trainers looking out onto the park with the blue sky and trees when her cousin called to say Iftikhar had died in 2020.

In 1987 Khushi, Zahra, and Zahra's little sister, returned to the family home in the UK. Mr. Hicks was with them, but he did not say much. Khushi did not have good English. So, Zahra and Jasmin would read. Zahra and Jasmin then did whatever they could to help.

Jasmin got married in 1991; she was eighteen. Neither Zahra nor Jasmin were particularly well-read; there were no professionals. For three years, it was only Khushi and Zahra. Then Zahra did all the reading, then Zahra took all the responsibility.

Zahra got married in 1993; she was twenty-one. She continued with responsibility.

In 1995, when a matter on a property got difficult. When there was no Google or information anywhere, Jasmin would have had her first children or was about to. Zahra had her first or second miscarriage. Zahra was working and studying, and she already had a difficult marriage.

Zahra gave Jasmin the good thing in London WC1, as they kept saying, "they want money." Zahra made sure her mother was safe, with income. Zahra took the terrible thing herself and all the claims and disrepair in Weston Super Mare, Avon.

Zahra took care of her family; she did the responsible thing, and her sister also said, "she was a victim."

Later, when a commercial value system was introduced, she said that is "not right." Zahra then had a hate campaign; her children were affected too. Zahra now knows she did not need to be so responsible. She could have taken the good thing, but she did not, as it would not be right.

In 2022 Camden WC1 is an expensive area in the UK, and Weston Super Mare is not. In 2022 the good thing is worth

£1.800,000; the terrible thing is £450,000. It could never be the same, not even in the past.

Fakher's home was first lost in 1986, and again in 1991, he had a hand too. It was Zahra that was confused by the old value system. Zahra thought you do business at work, not at home, plus she was simple in 1995.

With little knowledge or support, Zahra learned about responsibility, interpretation, and real estate.

Allah says do not take a good thing and replace it with bad, Quran 4:2. In 2022, when everyone that joined the hate campaign had a similar in their home, they said, "we could not do that with our parent's things; the money does not matter."

Each sister has a fragile relationship with the other; it is easily broken and has been the same for a long time.

Hold Me

Zahra found a picture of Princess Diana in Pakistan on the internet in November 2022.

The photo has Princess Diana in a green dress; she is dressed in shalwar kameez, a Pakistani dress. Princess Diana was in Pakistan, and behind her were Imran and Jemima Khan. It looks as if Princess Diana was in Pakistan.

Princess Diana died on 31 August 1997; the world mourned. On the day of Princess Diana's funeral, it was hot. Zahra lived in her dad's home. Her husband moved their mattress to the room where they sat as it was cooler. They lay on the floor and watched the funeral on a little TV; it was a sad day.

Mubarak Zahra's older sister says Fakher donated his shop in Liberty Market, Lahore, to the Imran Khan cancer hospital.

Mubarak said Imran Khan did meet them, but Fakher said, "no publicity," but Zahra does not know.

Zahra does know that everyone wanted Princess Diana's hairstyle then, and people also had bulimia.

All of Zahra's family history did impact her marriage. Zahra's husband had decency. He did not check out other women and did not interfere in Zahra's family affairs.

He was taller than Zahra, liked weightlifting, and was strong. He was more educated than Zahra's brothers-in-law. He was born in the UK and her brothers-in-law in Pakistan. His family always said he was only interested in you, no one else.

He used to talk about racism in the UK. Zahra does not know if that made his words strong and his attitude hard.

After four miscarriages, Zahra had her first son in 1998 and the other in 2001. Zahra wanted to give her sons the best possible start. Zahra put them in good nurseries and schools. Zahra worked two, sometimes three jobs.

The more she did, the less her husband did; in the end, she did everything herself. He did not want to take responsibility and was not always nice.

Then slowly, they lived separate lives. Once, she tried to get out of the house and could not. Zahra called the police and was two hours late for an interview. Zahra got the job.

When her dad died, she had to take her little son to the hospice; she placed him on the foot of her dead dad's bed. Then she left her husband and took the children with her.

When Zahra's husband had a heart attack, he held her hand and cried. When she got married, Zahra used to ask him to "hold her." It is odd how life works out.

It took 16 years for Zahra to get divorced, and he would not reply.

Allah says if a woman fears ill-treatment, it is ok to set things peacefully to right, Quran 4:128. In 2022 at a one YMCA event where she is a Trustee, someone talked about the importance of purpose and responsibility; Zahra thinks they are right, or people get sick.

But after Zahra's mother died, her family and community hated on her. As her children were affected too, her ex-husband would always be outside to ensure the children were safe, and his mum always on the phone. He told the children, "Your mother is right," based on her stance.

His family stood up and said, "she is our daughter; we will give her space," the elder uncle said to Zahra, "come and sit on my chair; you bought up our sons." Zahra's own family looked on.

Life is never black and white.

Professional Experience

During Zahra's 20 years in affordable housing, she bought much land, secured planning consent, and built thousands of new affordable homes.

In Local Government, she oversaw the Council's commercial portfolio for ten years and still dealt with affordable housebuilding from a land and strategy perspective.

Zahra has an old photo. It is taken from the top of a tall building; it shows a crane and a big construction project below.

The photo is of a new school being built when Zahra joined the London of Brent (LB Brent); she dealt with an old restrictive covenant that sterilised the land for 20 years and dealt with it in three months. Her work then released £40,000,000 from the priority school building programme to build a new school for 1.850 secondary-aged children. She was proud of her work.

The photo is from 2016; it is Zahra's photo. Zahra also sold the building she stood in; she visited it the day before the Council sold it. It was knocked down, and 248 new homes were built.

Zahra worked in Affordable Housing for 20 years, in Local Government for ten years, also Consultancy for four years.

Most of the people who gave Zahra a chance were white men. Mostly highly educated, intelligent, and skilled. Some were good men, and some went the extra mile. Zahra has done many roles, but some people stood out, and the associated roles are below.

In 1993 Zahra was a Rent Collector; this was her first housing job.

In 2002 after being two hours late for an interview, Zahra got the Project Managers jobs she had been one before. She bought land and built homes.

In 2007 the man from 2002 gave her a Development Manager role. He also made a case for funding the MBA in Construction and Real Estate.

In 2010 Zahra's MBA dissertation supervisor challenged her a lot; she liked him, and he had multiple doctorates.

In 2012 Zahra applied for a Head of Strategic Property job at a London Council, Brent. The Corporate Director gave her the job.

In 2017 Zahra's Royal Institution of Chartered Surveyors (RICS). The assessment of the Professional Competence (APC) Coach helped her.

In 2020 Zahra started her first consultancy job; a man from their client's team spotted her five years before.

Both men and women helped Zahra in separate ways; she likes to think she helped them too. In 2022 in the RICS's world community, of its 134,000 global members, Zahra believes it is as high as 84% men and 16% women. Zahra expects that is why men helped most, as there were very few women.

That is Zahra's 30 years of corporate real estate experience.

A Master's in Business Administration (MBA)

The College of Estate Management (CEM), now the University College of Estate Management (UCEM), took Zahra's photo in 2012. Zahra's picture was in their prospectus, she thinks, for three years.

A colleague that studied there later from LB Brent said Zahra's photo was also on the wall in the University. Prince Charles, their patron, was also in the Prospectus. Zahra never thought she would occupy the same space as the British Monarchy.

In 1987 Zahra got 5 GCSE grades A-C, she got English and Maths, and she went to Fulham Cross School in Fulham.

1995 Zahra did the Higher National Certificate in Housing at Hammersmith and West London College in Hammersmith. ASRA Greater London Housing Association paid for the course. Now just ASRA.

1996 Zahra did the Post Graduate Diploma in Management at Thames Valley University in Slough. ASRA paid for the course.

In 2011 Zahra completed MBA in Construction at Real Estate at the CEM. A Reading University Degree. Home Group paid for the course and the 2012 Diploma as a double degree. Zahra was a student representative for an international student community.

In 2012 CEM became a University of College of Estate Management, a significant moment in its 100+ years of history. Zahra is happy they did because, as a student representative, she said, "we would rather have a CEM degree."

In 2012 Zahra also got the Post Graduate Diploma in Project Management. A Reading University Degree.

In 2014 Zahra's Dissertation on Diversity in Construction was published by CEM as a short paper.

In 2012 when Jasmin asked, "why Zahra supports Mubarak?" Zahra supports her as she deserves a degree. She had good A' levels but could not go to university; she had a place. So, Mubarak worked and saved all her money to buy Zahra her first computer.

In 2018, Zahra met Malala Yousafzai when her eldest son was at the University of Oxford. What Malala says about girls' education is right; girls should have a right to education and complete it.

The Prophet Muhammad's wife, Ayesha, was one of Islam's most significant sources of knowledge and scholar. In 2022 Zahra expects the computer to be in a cupboard in Sialkot, Pakistan; from when they went there in 1986, they did not get to bring it back as they came back in a hurry.

That is Zahra's MBA is in Construction and Real Estate.

A Chartered Surveyor

The CEM in March 2014, published a paper on Diversity in Construction. The paper was a shortened version of Zahra's MBA dissertation on Diversity in Construction. The paper is still on CEM's website. In authoring her dissertation, Zahra learned the importance of being authentic.

Over the years, Zahra has held the following professional qualifications.

In September 2006, she became a Member of the Chartered Management Institute.

In March 2007, she became a Member of the Chartered Institute of Housing.

In May 2010, she became a Fellow of the Chartered Management Institute.

In July 2010, she became a Member of the Chartered Institute of Project Management.

In November 2012, she became a Member of the Chartered Institute of Building.

Zahra eventually stopped paying the annual fee for so many memberships as it was expensive.

In May 2017, Zahra became a Member of the Royal Institution of Chartered Surveyors. Zahra is a senior professional management consultant-chartered surveyor. There are only a few in the UK.

Of the Institution's 94,000 UK Member community. People with Pakistani heritage make up 0.001% of its members. Zahra is one of them.

While the MBA Zahra did was branded as an RICS-approved qualification. It did not automatically qualify her as an RICS Member.

To help, Zahra eventually found an APC Coach.

One day the coach came into the office at LB Brent to see Zahra. The coach saw the effect of a bullying incident. The coach gave her the confidence to raise a grievance.

A surveyor wanted Zahra to agree to a sale at £1,500,000, but Zahra did not agree. After he listened to Zahra, the council got £2,700,000 in the end. Even though Zahra was not a chartered surveyor then, her judgement was right. It was not just men that bullied. It was some women too.

In her last job, this old surveyor, a woman, would spend ages being hysterical over the phone; during the Covid lockdown, it was not pleasant to have all that in Zahra's home. Anyway, she retired after 42 years in the same place; it was good that she did as she was not in a healthy place.

In 2022 when a man incorrectly corrected Zahra for a word she used, she decided not to apply for a £120,000 per annum salary. Zahra is experienced and qualified and should not be corrected like a child and jobless in the UK today.

Leadership with a Vision

Zahra has a photo of LB Brent's Former Town Hall. When Zahra joined the Council in 2012, this was her first land sale. The old Grade II listed building was then restored. The building was repurposed and extended as a school.

The new school is for 1,650 secondary school-age children, and £50,000,000 was invested.

Only Zahra could get a sale of that size in contract in one month, and she did. LB Brent's Cabinet agreed to the sale in December 2012 and was in contract in January 2013. Through the marketing process, Zahra had lined up a seamless sale of a building of significant scale.

That was the month and year Zahra's mother died, but Khushi's death did not delay things.

Zahra envisioned a strong public service that could match the best in any sector. The Council previously outsourced many things, and Zahra upskilled her department and bought many tasks in-house. Zahra ran seven services at LB Brent in the end.

The Knowledge and Strategy team. Zahra worked with the service to deliver the asset management strategy; Zahra led. The Council portfolio was worth £1.5 bn. The strategy identified the potential for hundreds of new Council homes and £100,000,000's of new investment.

Zahra thinks the Council appointed her because of the 2011 Localism Act. The Act gave Councils new powers to invest. After three decades of no council housebuilding, they had an opportunity to build again but needed more in-house competency and skill.

As Zahra had a background in housebuilding, her appointment enabled the Council to realise its ambitions to build.

So, Zahra created the Council's Project Management function. Zahra created a new team from zero; there was a team of five in the end. But the growing program was worth again over £100,000,000.

The Property Service. Through a standardised approach, interest in the property increased. £100,000's was added to the annual rental value.

Property Buying. The team was responsible for buying in regeneration locations and temporary housing. The buying program was worth £150,000,000.

Again, Zahra created this team from zero, they did not exist before Zahra joined the Council, and with mostly non-chartered surveyors, it was a successful team and good value for money.

Facilities Management. The team managed operational buildings and LB Brent's new Civic Centre. When Zahra was there, the service significantly improved. The improvements in the catering service were significant, and they began to serve halal food as standard in line with the local market.

Then there was Health and Safety also Emergency Planning. Zahra did some particularly good work; her team did, too, and mostly supported her. Even the chartered surveyor that bullied her supported her in the end.

Zahra was told the department had to be restructured to a department as it was too big now, and she could apply for her job. Zahra's boss, a Black lady, said it had to do with a Local Government Policy. The policy did not feel fair at all, and Zahra felt upset.

The lady is now Chief Executive somewhere; she was an ambitious woman.

A Platform for Excellence

Zahra has a photo of the London Borough of Brent's New Civic Centre. The Council sold the Town Hall to pay for the new building. Hopkins Architects designed it. Skanska constructed it. The building opened in 2013. It is an Eco-friendly flagship new civic building with many facilities under one roof.

Zahra used to work in the building and was responsible for managing the building through one of her services, Facilities Management. Facilities management was responsible for day-to-day management. Zahra liked working here.

Zahra's little son would wait for her in the public areas, he did his homework in the building, and the man in Starbucks got to know him and gave him cookies with this drink. The Councillors also got to know Zahra's little son; the Deputy Leader would often stop to say hello to him.

After Zahra became a chartered surveyor, Zahra said to her staff, "as I have got through, you should try too," She said, "do not give up if your get referred; I did but kept on trying."

Each month, Zahra began to hold monthly RICS coaching sessions. All staff in her department and then others started to join too. The approach meant that the department began working similarly.

The RICS process is structured. It looks carefully at the method. It standardises the approach with everyone working the same way. It focused on good casework and building technical expertise. The department took industry guidance and converted it into practical policies considering how the Council worked.

After Zahra left LB Brent, two members of her former staff became chartered. The first was a British Black man with Nigerian heritage. He had two daughters, and he always thanked Zahra. He is MRICS now.

The other is someone from a very deprived area of LB Brent. He was a little tricky due to his background, but he listened to Zahra. He later became AssocRICS and is a Registered Valuer now. He says that his life would be quite different without Zahra's guidance. He has since had two daughters too.

At LB Brent, when the £130,000,000 property buying program was audited. As staff followed policies they had designed and were given. The auditor had no recommendations for Zahra's area. It was good to see her approach and internal processes work.

Zahra had many colleagues and friends in LB Brent; while she did not plan a leaving event, many people came up to give her cards and presents. Her department put on a leaving lunch; it was 12 February 2018, a few days before Valentine's Day, so the tables were all red.

Many people that worked under Zahra have since progressed.

A Scheme to be Most Proud Of.

Zahra has a photo is of a new regeneration location called One Public Estate (OPE) Northwick Park in LB Brent, Northwest London. Network Homes will build the first homes. PRP Architects designed it. Vistry will build the first phase.

In the end, Northwick Park will provide 2,400 new homes; Zahra estimates £370,000,000 to be invested in the local area over 10 to 15 years. It is big. The London Borough of Brent secured £530,500 of OPE Funding, the maximum award; Zahra led the bid, which the Council approved.

The Council had the opportunity to bid for OPE funding. The OPE Programme is a government-led initiative by the Cabinet Office also the Local Government Association. The Programme encourages Public Sector Landowners to work together to optimise land.

The OPE theory is that marriage will enable a more significant outcome.

Under Zahra's leadership, with the help of a Project Manager, the Council secured OPE funding. This helped bring landowners together.

The Council's land ownership comprised metropolitan open land and a golf club. Next door was Northwick Park Hospital. Then also Westminster University. Network Homes were the fourth major landowner, also other less significant parcels of land.

Through a carefully thought-through process. Drawing on Zahra's two decades of project management and delivery experience. As well as knowledge of Local Government and Public Services. And careful relationship management. Zahra pulled together the partnership agreement, which all partners signed.

Zahra then sought professional advice. She worked carefully to ensure all partners had an equal voice, and each partner's input was sought on the scope of services and the final appointments. The outcome was a first-site capacity study, feasibility study, and delivery plan. The night Zahra left; the Council approved moving to the next steps.

On 12 February 2018, a report went to the Council's Cabinet on OPE Northwick Park. Zahra asked the Chief Executive "if they had any issues with the published report?" They said, "no, your judgement was right." They were rightly worried about a scheme of such a size; it was seamlessly put together.

The Chief Executive also said, "are you sure about where you are going next?" Zahra was not; she was sad to leave. It was a strange question from the Chief Executive as she thought they did not want Zahra to work there. She gave Zahra the impression that they did not trust her judgement before.

But Northwick Park was an odd site, as communication was carefully managed; rather than the Council approaching the market, the market began to approach the Council, and it was only then that the Council realised what Zahra worked on was of significant scale.

As most of Zahra's work was seamlessly delivered, it was easy to think she did not do anything. Zahra worked long hours in LB Brent; sometimes, when she left, she hoped people would not see her as it was so late that it was embarrassing.

Zahra respected this Chief Executive, but misunderstandings are not good things.

Zahra was happy on what she achieved at Northwick Park.

Fellowship

Zahra thinks the Board Room at the RICS Headquarters in Westminster, London is nice. It is covered in brown wood, with old paintings, and at the front, all the names of past presidents are listed. The roof is all white with spotlights and white carpet on the floor.

Zahra worked hard to become a member of the RICS.

In her new job, Zahra transformed a department that was failing. It had very low performance. Some people were not coming to work.

The organisation provided services to two London Councils. Zahra managed four real estate services. Strategic Asset Management, Project Management, Property, and Valuation, also Facilities Management. The department had 130 members of staff.

As Zahra did before, she delivered a full review of the Property Portfolio. Zahra personally wrote both Council's Asset Management Strategy and Plan. The combined portfolio value was £5bn. Zahra also secured £300,000 of OPE funding to review one Council's Town Hall site.

But here it was, sad. One person tried to take their life as they did not like when restructure proposed that they apply for their job. Zahra worked hard to keep them, and they said "thank you" to Zahra through their manager. They were sad, just like Zahra was when she left her last job.

Then when another director had a similar matter with their staff, Zahra left that job. The place was not very well; it was not good for Zahra.

When Zahra left, one supplier that had worked with a Council said, "the service had been the best in ten years." Staff in her department were told "not to change anything and to do as Zahra did as it represented best practice."

Zahra liked the line manager who said goodbye; he said Zahra was "very brave," although she was not too sure about him.

Drawing on all the work Zahra has done. All her professional experience. Qualifications. Professional Body Membership. Her work on various Boards. Zahra's published dissertation on Diversity. Also, Senior Leadership.

Zahra was delighted to be fast-tracked and approved as a Fellow of the RICS. It has been hard too.

This job taught Zahra that we all have limits, even "brave people."

It is nice that Zahra is now a Fellow of the RICS and one of only 4% of women Fellows. Had she not been so resilient, she doubts she would have that status today.

Allyship

Zahra has a photo of an empty office in a new building. A man bullied his boss out of a job, but he did a particularly good job emptying the office floor. It was all ready for a new tenant to move in on time. Zahra went to see what he did in 2019. Zahra took the photo then. Zahra left that job in 2021.

As Zahra just wanted to work. One thing she could have improved at was building Allyship.

So, in her last job, when this white man bullied another white man out of a job. While Zahra personally wrote their client Council's Asset Management Strategy, their portfolio was worth £1.5bn.

Also, people used to say we have seen more of you in six weeks than we did of the past Director in three years. Instead of dealing with the bully man, they began to pick on Zahra, and she left. They paid Zahra £121,000 each year.

The job before, there was a man that had an affair; he caused all sorts of problems for Zahra. Zahra's son said that as he had travelled all over Europe, "they are racist where he comes from," so he targeted Zahra.

The other problem was the line manager that could not manage stress; he left and said, "sorry." It was the same with the man who bullied her before; he got away with it as he had a special relationship with a senior person.

Zahra also learned that while some Members may like you when it comes to standing up for you, they will not.

As David Lammy MP says in his book on "Tribes," people are tribal. People look after themselves first or their friends. In the elected member's case, they have not been equipped to challenge clever policy arguments, as some can come from the same background as Zahra.

Rishi Sunak, the 2022 UK Prime Minister, and Sadiq Khan, the London Mayor, are a new generation. Others fought in a more tribal manner.

Zahra did build Allyship when she had a piece of work; look at what she did on One Public Estate Northwick Park. She felt very unsettled after leaving that job.

Zahra learned to value herself and walk away when things were not healthy.

Chapter 4. Hajj

Picture an outdoor beach, a few clouds, a blue sky, sand, and sea. It is a warm summer's day on a traditional English beach.

This is West Wittering Beach, UK. Zahra and Jasmin went together, Rahma went too, and Zahra sent Salman a photo.

In 2023 Zahra hopes Mubarak may come too, also her two sons and everyone's children. Zahra took such a photo in August 2022. It was after Zahra came back from Hajj.

An Oxford University Graduate.

Zahra has a picture on one of her walls at home. It shows a man sitting behind a table and a lady standing beside him. On the other side of the table, is a man standing up; behind him are a few other men. They all have old-fashioned English clothes.

Underneath the picture is the words, "The hopes of the family, an admission at the University."

Zahra's elder son got an A* for his Art GCSE. In primary school, his teacher and Zahra used to say he "has no talent in Art." His work used to be quite dark, but later it became very beautiful, and Zahra's son proved them wrong. He went to one of the best Grammar Schools in the UK; he liked school.

He once told his primary school teacher, "he just wants to make his mum proud."

So, Zahra's elder son went to the University of Oxford. The World's Best University. Her elder son is an academic. He got 100% A or A*'s at A 'level. At GCSE, he got 100% A or A*s.

Zahra's little son. He did very well too. He is a very caring, considerate, and kind man. He studies at Queen Mary's University. He did well at A 'levels and GCSEs too. He was born on 9/11 the year the twin towers came down in the United States, it was a strange time then.

Zahra's elder son says, "mum find your own identity." Zahra was a little confused. Zahra's children gave her real purpose. But when he said, "mum, you do not even know me." He was right, too, because she did not see that he had become a grown-up man. He was ready to be independent.

As a single parent, Zahra did the best for her beautiful little sons. If nothing else, Zahra gave her sons the best possible start and good education. Zahra is grateful to Allah that she had two lovely children. She is proud of them.

Allah also says your wealth and children are your biggest test Quran 64:15. In 2012, Zahra reflected a lot and looked at lots of family photos, and she can only see that she had an enjoyable time with her sons. While Zahra did a lot, her first and primary consideration was her children.

Family problems and work issues affected the home, too; Covid has been awful for many families. All that to one side, providing for children is the father's responsibility; it is not the sole obligation of the mother. Zahra cannot and could not force anyone.

Infaq is an Arabic word to mean spending and disbursement, but it also carries the sense of doing so to please Allah without asking for any favour or hoping for a return. The word infaq is mentioned in the Quran in 17:100.

One son came to see Zahra before she went to Hajj, and one did not.

It was a privilege to bring up two lovely young men; the rest now down to them. Zahra did her best, you cannot expect grown men to be children, it is unattractive too, for men that cannot stand on their own.

Maintain Ties of Kinship

Zahra has a photo of a lady sitting on a sofa with nice green clothes; it looks like she is dressed for a wedding. She has a long green dress and head scarf to match; it has gold embroidery work.

In her hand is a lovely black handbag. Zahra knows it was an original Versace, as she used to buy such bags in the past. She still has the bag at home, although she no longer uses such bags.

A few years back, Zahra went to a wedding, she dressed like that, and no one except her sons wanted to sit next to her, also a few elders from the family, her cousins, and the hosts.

So, while everyone ran away, Zahra sat on stage and asked her son to take her photo. Her cousins said, "you look lovely with a headscarf," so she put it on. It is Zahra's photo from, say, 2018.

Before Iftikhar died, he used to say to Zahra, "let me see your face." Zahra used to think that was odd as everyone said, "you look like your father," and when they said it then, Zahra did not know they meant it nicely. But when Iftikhar said it, he meant it nicely; his daughters say he meant it nicely.

Iftikhar died a few years back during the Covid pandemic. In 2020 the UK Government said only thirty people could attend a funeral. Iftikhar had seven children, five daughters, two sons, and many grandchildren, mostly young men; they hardly had any space. They said Zahra to come, so she went with her elder son; she felt welcome.

In 2022 when Zahra hurt her hand before Ramadan. Mubarak, her big sister, said, "I did not sleep all night as I worried about you." Jasmin also said, "it is wrong that you do not turn on the heating, turn it on as it is cold," as Zahra is not working, she wants to manage her costs. But no one will feel for you like your own family.

When people were not friendly to Zahra, each Eid, she bought sweets or meat and gave them to people who would not speak to her. Allah does say to maintain ties of kinship, Quran 4:1.

So while it was not pleasant, people did not want to sit next to Zahra; in the end, like Khushi lost her sight when Jasmin and Zahra were twenty-three, they were blind women then, neither was read in 1995 and things happened that were not right.

Like Allah Zahra's father said in 1993. "Whenever you are together, you will always find me there, but if you split, you will find emptiness. Try to be together often," he was right.

Later, Zahra realised it was OK for no one to sit next to her; sometimes, that was best. It gives freedom to develop and look at the work Zahra did in ten years. It also allows one proper time to reflect. Independence is good.

Both sisters came to see Zahra off to Hajj.

Zahra's Hajj

The Kaabah, which Muslims believe to be the house of God surrounded by pilgrims. The Kaabah is in Masjid e Haram in Makkah, Saudi Arabia. Zahra took the photo of the Kaabah in July 2022. The Kaabah was full of pilgrims in ihram circling the Kaabah as they did tawaf.

Ihram is simple clothing, two white sheets for men and modest Islamic women's clothing. Tawaf is circling the Kaabah seven times.

On 2 July, Zahra arrived in Makkah in Ihram; she stayed in the Fairmont Clock Tower Hotel; while everyone else shared, she managed to get a room to herself; she stayed 12 days in one of the best hotels.

On 2 July, when she arrived in Ihram, Zahra did all her tawaf and umrah.

Umrah is the intention; it is to wear ihram, do tawaf, walk between the mountains of Safa and Marwah seven times, and cut or shave one's hair. To drink Zamzam water and holy water.

On 7 July, from 8th Dhu al Hijjah, she went to the Mina camps to do as the Prophet Muhammad did. Zahra stayed five nights; she returned to Makkah every day in the daytime. She stayed in the most VIP camps, 40B.

Mina means to be put to the test. Muslims believe that Mina is connected to the test Allah put on Prophet Ibrahim to when he was told to sacrifice his son. Mina is the place where he was tested.

On 8 July, the day of Arafah. It was hot in the Arafah camps. There Zahra slept a lot, which she should not have, but she could not get up. Zahra did get up when these tribal Arab women came and sat in her camp.

The Mount of Arafah is where the Prophet Muhammad delivered the last sermon. It is known as the "Mountain of Mercy."

On 8 July, the evening after the Maghreb prayer, the group went to Muzdalifah camps. Zahra was scared as it was dark, with one million people in one place. She walked with a man from

Rwanda, who spoke English as he was based in the US; he said she was the "bravest woman he knew."

To stay one night under the open sky represents equality and seeking repentance from Allah.

On 8 and 9 July, Zahra stayed all night in the outdoor camp at Muzdalifah on the soil with many people; she had a sleeping bag on the floor and placed her umbrellas around for privacy.

On 9 July, at Muzdalifah with an Egyptian lady and her family of twelve people, Zahra read Fajr at the train station and left the area. Zahra then went to Jamarat.

Jamarat is a symbolic place for the first three days of stoning; this is where Prophet Ibrahim (Abraham) is believed to have been tested, and three times, he threw a stone at the devil.

On 9 July, a family paid Zahra's bus fare to Makkah; she had no money. This was Eid day 2022.

When Zahra arrived in Makkah, it was Eid day, and after being in camps and out all night, they came as if we were the poorest people in the world. It was very humbling. Later in the day, Zahra got an email to say Qurbani (a sacrifice) had been done.

Zahra's Hajj ritual was complete.

After Eid 2022.

Zahra hears that Hajj is the only religious ritual that was started by the footsteps of a woman and the journey of Hajar, the wife of Prophet Ibrahim, as she ran backward and forwards looking for water for her thirsty son, Prophet Ismael.

The Prophet Muhammad is buried in the Prophets Mosque in Madinah. Madinah was called Yathrib before, but the name was changed after the Prophet arrived. Someone sent Zahra the photo on WhatsApp as her phone was broken. Zahra has an image from July 2022.

After Eid day, Zahra managed to return to Mina each day from Makkah, it was hard to leave a five-star hotel and go and stay in the camps all night, but she did. Zahra saw a few Tablighi jamaat (preachers) women off in the camps. Zahra kept going back for the prescribed three days.

Zahra took advantage of the fact that she was alone.

The first day of stoning in Jamarat was on Eid day and 9 July 2022.

10 July 2022 was the second day of stoning in Jamarat.

11 July was the third day of stoning in Jamarat.

As Zahra was a woman on her own, the Hajj book she had said it was OK for Zahra to do stoning when it was not busy. Zahra used to go first thing after Fajr or late after everyone had been. She preferred to go after Fajr, and then she would go to Makkah for the day.

While others struggled to get around, Zahra managed to, and on the last day, a kind Arab man who was walking the same way helped her get back to Makkah, she was a bit afraid as he was not sure, but he was OK. There were no buses that day first thing in the morning.

From 12 July, Zahra no longer had to go to the Mina camps, and she finished. Zahra got a temperature, slept for 24 hours, and struggled to get up and do her final tawaf before leaving for Madinah.

Zahra had the best hajj, and the eight days in Madinah from 13 July enabled her to get better before travelling back to the UK on 22 July; she came back from Jeddah. Even in Madinah, she had her own room.

One day she walked straight into Rawdah, where the Prophet Muhammad is buried; many people could not go and then left. There was an online ticket booking system, which some said took much work to navigate and book on.

Salman and Zahra's big Sufi sister were with her the whole time; before going, she tried to make good with everyone, and it was nice that most people tried back.

Mubarak sought her out when they thought she had gone missing as her mobile phone broke while away. Zahra was very tearful that day, and she was grateful Mubarak called.

On 22 July 2022, Zahra returned to the UK; Jasmin and her family were at the airport to collect Zahra. Jasmin had lots of flowers; Zahra was happy she came.

Zahra had lost much weight, dropping to 47kg; she asked Jasmin not to take any photos.

Reorientation after coming back to the UK has been challenging. At Hajj, everyone only has one aim; in everyday life, people do not. It has taken Zahra are while to start to find her feet again.

Board Member

Zahra has a screenshot of the RICS's LinkedIn post in November 2022; it shows Zahra when she went to Hajj in July 2022.

Zahra is dressed in a blue head-to-toe modest long dress; as the dress is so long, she holds it in her hand against her chest; as she does that, she looks into the camera and takes a selfie of herself.

Behind Zahra is the Kaabah and the house of Allah, and people walk around doing tawaf.

Zahra does not think the RICS has ever posted such an article. Zahra authored the article when she came back from Hajj.

Zahra is a member of the RICS World UK & Ireland Board. The article got the second most likes on the RICS LinkedIn post for a month. It got nine hundred likes. Only Rishi Sunak, the UK's new Prime Minster, got more. Rishi got 2,500 likes.

In December 2022, the Board Chairperson told Zahra that she "had become an overnight celebrity;" he says pleasant things a lot, and Zahra likes him.

In 2022 Zahra became a Board Member of the RICS World UK & Ireland Board. The Chairperson interviewed her; he said, "you do not need us as a brand; you have your brand." Zahra thought she had given the wrong answer. He was kind; he works for a significant UK Property Consultancy.

In 2022 Zahra became the Chair of one YMCA's Development Board. The Chair of the main board was a lovely man and the same with the Chief Executive. Zahra is a Trustee for them too. Zahra will report to a Bishop in the future as he is their new Chair. The bishop oversees 150 Parishes.

In 2022 Zahra completed a 6-year term with Southern Housing Group on their Development Committee.

Six years before, when Zahra interviewed for the Southern, the old Chief Executive heard her name. He said "not to make her wait and to give her the part;" staff said they would anyway. Zahra also likes the Chair of the now-merged Southern Housing Group.

Zahra is now looking for a similar Board role as her term with Southern has ended.

As recently as one hundred years ago. Women in UK society did not work. Many South Asian women still do not work. Like migrants, few women were doing corporate jobs.

Real estate and construction were and are still seen as "men's work." People say to Zahra; you are not in an easy profession. But Zahra has always enjoyed her work. Why Allah put Zahra in this profession only, he knows.

Zahra also said, "it is not her photo people like as people do not know her." She thinks people like "that the Profession and UK are changing." It goes back to her 2011 dissertation, which the CEM published on diversity. The paper said, "diversity is our strength." It is also said to be authentic.

It goes back to what Allah has said, "I made you man and woman, I made you tribes and nations, to get to know each other" Quran 49:13. We are all human beings. It is people that have created differences.

After Zahra's dissertation, she did not see who she was as a barrier; she saw her identity as an opportunity; she applied for roles as she thought she could do them and add value to organisations.

So far, it has served Zahra well.

Before Hajj

Zahra has a Quran. It says the English translation is completed at the Custodian of the Two Holy Mosques King Fahd Complex for the Printing of the Holy Quran. Al Madinah Al-Munawarah Under the Auspices of the Ministry of Hajj and Endowments. The Kingdom of Saudi Arabia 1413 AH.

In June 2022, when Zahra thought, she was going to Hajj, she had an emotional journey to accept that she was going alone. She was then told she could not go by Dome Tours, as the system had changed. Zahra was quite upset.

The day she was informed she had agreed to meet the to be new President of the RICS in Central London Mosque; although the President could not come, the brothers in the Mosque said to Zahra, "we have a present for you."

The brothers gave Zahra the Quran from the holiest mosques in Makkah and Madinah. It is not for sale.

When Zahra showed Rahma what the Mosque had given her, she said, "that is the Quran they used to give pilgrims after they completed Hajj." Zahra does not know if that is correct.

But Zahra did say then, "as the process even before going had been so emotional, she feels as if she has done Hajj without going and that she was content with whatever Allah decides."

Zahra is grateful Allah decided that she does Hajj.

After returning from Hajj, while people say, "you are a new-born baby, and you have been cleansed," it is sometimes hard to stay on track because you get pulled in all directions.

Zahra can only try, like everyone, to stay on the right track.

Zahra hopes Allah accepts her, Hajj; she will not use the name Hajjan for this reason, as only Allah knows whose Hajj is accepted.

Ten years ago, Zahra started to fast, go to Taraweeh, and attend Central London Mosque in the UK. Although since coming back from Hajj, she has not gone for a while, nor has she gone to her dad's grave, she should.

Zahra has a special connection with the Central London Mosque.

Chapter 5. Reflection

Picture a big chandelier; it is the biggest in the UK. The chandelier sits in the middle of a giant circle dome.

The top of the ceiling is light blue, and the bottom has assorted colours of blue and yellow, a mosaic design. There are also spotlights. Underneath the base of the dome is gold with black writing. The writing is in Quranic Arabic and verses of the Quran. It is in a mosque.

The mosque's walls are white; underneath is dark and light blue carpet and Islamic prayer mats. Zahra also started her Hajj journey here.

When her mother died in 2013, her immediate family and community stopped talking to her. While things were terrible, Zahra used to go to the Central London Mosque in Regents Park, UK. Zahra has many images of the men's area below, as she took the photos from the woman's section upstairs.

Zahra likes this mosque a lot; maybe it was Allah's way of opening his door.

Be Fair to Children

Zahra has a picture of what looks like an old home, an old person's home, and a person that is now dead. Zahra expects that it may have one day been someone's family home, but to Zahra, it looks all empty now.

It seems as if not only have the people died but all their old memories were taken away too. That is Zahra's photo from many years back.

To Zahra, that looks like her old family home where she grew up.

Zahra remembers her mother Khushi would have walked around a place like that. She would have woken up and opened the curtains. Zahra used to sleep on the top floor; she liked the little room the most.

In the basement lived an old man, Mr. Hicks. Zahra's dad used to sleep on the top floor in the big bedroom.

Fakher used to keep the house simple. When Fakher lived there, it was never broken or damp; he used to take care of the home Zahra expects Fakher worked extremely hard to make a place like that.

When Khushi was almost blind, she used to struggle. When Zahra went, she knew she would be tired, and Zahra was the old child she used to cook for in the end. Sometimes the food would get a little burnt, but it was OK as Zahra was hungry and had not eaten all day.

Khushi was unread, she needed help to understand, and while she tried to be fair, she needed clarification on what fair meant; she was no property valuer, and she had no idea about real estate work, but she knew family history.

Allah has said to be fair to children, Quran 4:11. Fakher and Khushi said we want to be fair. When Fakher left in 1985, he did what was fair, and then it was down to Khushi, Zahra, and Jasmin.

Allah says if you fear injustice to speak, Quran 4:9 as that is best for those that live but also those that are dead, and that is right.

When things happen when you do not know, that is different. Later, when Zahra and Jasmin did know to hide behind Khushi, a blind unread woman was wrong. Fakher dealt with Mubarak differently.

When you go to Hajj, they say it is a mini version of the day of judgement; they say people will only be concerned with themselves. Life is the same, people have choices, and we all have two paths, but your first home is your most powerful school.

Like everyone in the community still lives in their family home, Fakher's family should be too. As a single woman, a Muslim family is responsible for looking after her, but no one does.

Zahra showed Jasmin what she wrote, and she said, "take me out of your book," but Zahra said, "it is not about you; it is about a person called Jasmin, also my journey, and if you did not like what Jasmin did, why did you do it?"

Zahra has no reply but does not expect an invite for Christmas 2022. Also, other people's position is not sustainable; they will have to do something one day.

Zahra has learned that one should do as the Prophet Muhammad and deal with such matters before death if possible; it is not always doable.

The Son of David

Zahra has a photo of a man prostrating, bowing down on the street. The man has a sign in his hand; it says I am "I am hungry." The man also has a plastic cup in front; it is to collect money. This is Kensington High Street, in West London. It is one of London's most expensive areas. This was in 2022. This is Zahra's photo; many homeless people are in London.

The man is wearing a black jacket and track bottoms with a big white stripe on the site; he also has black trainers. Behind him is a bus stop and in front of a shop window. His knees, elbows, and hands are on the floor. His head is also touching the floor; it is quite a dark photo. Zahra walked past the man, and then she returned to him.

Zahra said, "get up off the floor." She told him, "Let me buy you food." She took him to Ranoush Restaurant on Kensington High Street. She said, "tell me what you want to eat?" She ordered his food and said, "they will give it to you. But never let me see you bow like that on the street again." Zahra said, "you only bow like that to Allah." She said, "do not do it again."

Zahra met this other young man in Central London Mosque. Zahra said to the mosque people, "can you not, see? He is homeless." They said, "no," he was "OK." She said, "he is not." So, she was going to take him to find his things. The brothers then came after Zahra. They said, "let us deal with him." The Brothers did. Since then, they have changed their approach and policy.

Zahra also met this other young man. An orthodox Jewish man. You could see he was with the way he conducted himself. But he said, "I am not religious." He said, "I have been bought up in an orthodox environment." He said, "I am the bloodline of David." Zahra does not know what this means; she looked it up, and it goes back to Prophet David and Jesus.

He said, "you are a good woman," and prayed for Zahra. "May God put right all that is wrong." The Son of David later texts Zahra to say, "I am just a homeless man." Zahra said, "she would meet him and take him to Central London Mosque to see if the brothers could help him too." She did not see him again.

All Three homeless men left an impression on Zahra because all our destinies could be different; Muslims believe all our Qadr was written 50,000 years before the heavens and earth were created. Allah decides each person's Qadr. Qadr is Fate, Predestination, and Decree of Allah.

At Hajj, you see many Black, brown, and white people from everywhere on a big scale. But who decides where each person is born, who is rich, and who is poor?

Wherever Allah placed you, he put you there for a reason; it is your responsibility to make the most of where you live and what you have.

Coping Mechanism

Zahra put a photo in a word document; the auto text said, "a woman is holding a cigarette;" Zahra does not know who she is. She is a young white woman with a t-shirt that says, "hope." She is pretty; she has dark colour long hair, no make-up, and she is beautiful without make-up.

Zahra does like the music she plays; it has a nice rhythm. Zahra took that photo from YouTube in November 2022. Women smoking is taboo, but when you overload a person, they must cope. Many Brits do not care, but many South Asians do, the same in some Black Muslim communities.

Due to Covid 19 in 2020, many University age children were sent home with little or no notice. Parents that previously went to work were forced to work at home. Zahra's household was the same.

Initially, it was fun, but slowly, the realisation hit: no one was used to being home like this. Many households were put under pressure, and nationally in the UK, domestic incidents went up. Many had family breakdowns, including challenges between parents and their children.

One of Zahra's friends says, "it is as if she has lost two adult children." She said she "first tried to be busy, then realised she was grieving, and now she takes each day, one day at a time."

Some of Zahra's sisters do not go to work. They talk about taking sleeping pills to get away; they want to sleep, and some talk about suffering from depression, even the happy ones.

Zahra has been at home for three years; she is still determining if working like before will work for her. Zahra is starting to recreate how she works; she has been happy working on her book. Similar work would be nice.

Only a few people exist in what has become a virtual world for Zahra. Sometimes it is like it is only the homeless man and woman when she goes out. Zahra cannot help everyone, so taking a break has been good.

What is a normal person? Many people use coping mechanisms. Even at Hajj, this poor sister said, "I cannot give up here, too; I wish I could." But people do their best. We ought not to judge another person. If what they do, does not affect you or others, turn a blind eye.

By December 2020, the UK started to roll out the national Covid vaccination programme, which helped. But some relationships are still broken. Cover and forgive each other as the Prophet Muhammad would.

Zahra has learned that people are only human; no one is perfect.

Chapter 6. Know Yourself

Zahra has this beautiful photo of a human-sized white wedding dress; it has silver sequins on the front, a shoulder less dress, and a big round bottom that is higher at the front and touches the floor at the back. The bottom of the dress has flowers all over.

The photo is of a piece of art, a paper mâché dress. Zahra's elder son made that for his art GCSE in 2015.

When Zahra returned from work, he would say, "mum help me make the paper flowers." So, Zahra and her son would make them together. He also made an art book on dampness, as they lived in a damp house. It made Zahra smile; kids can see opportunity in many things.

Zahra used to take her sons to many fashion shows and lovely places. Both Zahra's sons know about fashion and good things.

Zahra thinks the paper dress is excellent; her younger son makes delicious cupcakes.

Respect Your Roots.

Zahra's photo is of a person sitting at a desk. She has short brown hair, looks straight at the camera, and looks like she is in her twenties or thirties. She is wearing a white dress with different coloured flowers. Behind her are a sofa and green curtains. She is very pretty; she has a medium build.

This was Queen Elizabeth II when she was young; Zahra does not know how old she is; she looks young and wonderful. The Queen died when she was age 96. She died on 8 September 2022. As Zahra could, she went to all the Queen's events. Zahra could make a book on this too.

When Zahra read the tributes, many people said, "thank you to the Queen for giving them a home in the UK and a better life than they had from wherever they came. Plenty of women were killed in Iran in 2022 for not wearing a headscarf properly.

The Queen and Fakher would have been born in 1926, which is almost one hundred years, and since then, much has changed in the UK.

The two thousand eleven census results showed. Few people were getting married, and marriage had lost its sanctity. Many people were cohabiting. People had smaller families due to effective contraception. More people were getting divorced. The role of women had changed significantly. Same-sex marriages were permitted. More women are educated.

We operate on a global platform; travel has increased, and the internet and virtual world is business as usual daily. Adoption laws allow single people and couples to now apply. Religious values have changed; in 2022, research showed that less than 50% of the UK is now Christian, the lowest number ever.

South Asian people born and bought up in the UK are changing too, and as children go to school together, their mindset is becoming the same, so changes in Britain are affecting all communities.

Zahra has enjoyed the privilege of education and the right to work in the UK and progress, she has stood equal, but not identical to men, and despite many challenges, she did well. In contrast, in South Asian cultures, she would have been written off a long time ago. Zahra is grateful for the privilege she enjoyed as a British-born citizen.

When she looks back, the system paid for her education. The work she did, she could not do in Pakistan, although from her cousins in Pakistan, she can see change there too. In 2022, Zahra's younger cousins are highly educated women in Pakistan. They have Ph.D. s, Masters, and Doctorates.

For many women, both South Asian and others, it is a shame that equal rights later felt like a reverse abuse of rights, where women do more. Zahra often talks to other women about this because she and they do all the work.

From the example of the Prophet Muhammad, Muslims are responsible for contributing, integrating, and being part of society wherever they live. In 2022 Zahra likes that she is part of UK society.

Slowly, she finds more non-South Asian friends and enjoys their company; she even made a friend sitting in Piccadilly when the Queen died, a white lady that had just lost her 28-year-old son. Zahra understood her grief.

A mix of diverse cultures and people is lovely, Zahra likes it, and there is this new emerging British Muslim identity; it is different from people living in Pakistan.

Know Your Rights and Responsibilities

A picture containing roses is from Pakistan in the UK; it is Zahra's friends. It is common for Pakistan to use derogatory remarks and other methods to control Zahra, even police threats. Still, her dad said, "it is OK," she will see as it has gotten better after she said, "stop being an idiot."

The roses are homegrown, Pakistan says, "they are older than both of us," Zahra expects Pakistan's dad may have planted them.

Before Pakistan's dad died, Zahra felt something was going to happen; she told of two dreams she had; Pakistan reacted as if they feared her. Pakistan's dad died that week, and Zahra had never met him; she has never been invited to visit the roses.

In the workplace, careful monitoring of Zahra's grammar creates false legitimacy and power-driven by ego. In 2022 Zahra learned to say, "do not be silly; I am an educated woman of substance."

Investigations in the London Fire Brigade 2022 say, "there is a deeply misogynistic and racist culture in the public body." Jaden was based in one of London's most deprived and diverse boroughs. In 2020, the suicide of Jaden Matthew Francois Espirit, a Black man, triggered an investigation.

In 2022, Nazir Afzal OBE, the investigating officer, says, "it is a pandemic." Zahra thinks Nazir is correct, but for South Asian women, that can be misogyny in your own home too, and from women.

Zahra is fifty. Her first responsibility is to herself now.

Her responsibility to her children is now that they stand on their own feet and start looking after their mum.

For Jasmin, she did plenty when Zahra was responsible. There is much history. Life is about give and take, and if, after taking silently and by force, there was a hate campaign against Zahra in 1993 and 2012. She could not give even a little back after Zahra asked; there was nothing she could do.

In terms of her elder sister, Mubarak, her responsibility is to give her respect and to expect care and love back; she is her big sister.

Someone the other day said, "Zahra, it was you; you made sure your mum was safe. Otherwise, she would have been a homeless woman because everyone else said to leave your home, but you said not to." Even when she died, Zahra recalls she did the same and said, "no, do not go."

In the Quran, Allah has said it is a man's duty to provide for his family, the Quran 4:34. It is not for a woman to do everything alone or for husbands to send their wives to their mother's homes to go and fight for money or against their sister, it is none of their business.

A woman should encourage men to progress and provide but also have a backup plan.

With charity, Zahra used to help, and then she learned her assistance was crippling households, so she stopped; now, she uses the skill she has and works for the public good, books such as this, which will be her legacy.

If nothing else, Zahra wronged herself, but she did OK; look after yourself. Zahra tells all the men to now pay, and she tells all the young women and girls she meets to do the same.

Find Your Own Identity.

Like Zahra's son's beautiful paper Mâché dress, Zahra authored a dissertation, and she got a distinction in 2011 and an MBA from Reading University.

The College of Estate Management then published her work. It was a very good piece of work. Zahra's dissertation was on diversity in the UK construction industry.

In 2022, while she thinks some things may have changed, she also thinks some may not have changed, and, in her case, she has reached her "glass ceiling." Zahra does not know, but as she said, she should be working. Zahra works as is her habit, which is what this book is about.

Zahra has many firsts; she is the first British-born Muslim woman of Pakistani heritage to do many things.

Zahra is the first woman to sit on the RICS World UK & Ireland Board, representing 94,000 members; she is the first to write on Hajj for them.

Zahra is the first such woman to be a Trustee of one YMCA, an old Christian charity; it is 154 years old and served 94,000 people in 2019.

Zahra was the first woman to sit on Southern Housing Group's development Board for six years; they house over 30,000 people.

Zahra is one of the first such women to be a Fellow of the RICS; only 4% of their Fellow community are women, and of the 94,000 members, only 177 (0.0019%) are Pakistani heritage; they are likely to be mostly men.

Zahra is the first such woman to independently, with the help of one person in her team, see the potential of One Public Estate Northwick Park, a new £370,000,000, 2,400 home new regeneration.

Zahra was one of the first such women to hold a Chief Property Officer's post in a Local Government; she was the authorising officer on property transactions of up to £1,000,000.

Zahra likes to think she had a small role in changing RICS's 100+ year history when she said, "change from Chairman to Chair." The same in CEM's 100+ year plus history, she said, "apply for university status yourself," which they then got in 2012.

Zahra is one of the first such women to have a 30-year career in corporate real estate and one of the only rent collectors' tenants who wanted to do a petition to keep; she worked at William Sutton Housing then in 1993.

They liked Zahra as she read for them as she did for her mum; some of the angriest tenants were illiterate.

Allah lifts whom he pleases; Zahra is not sure why she, Salman, and Rahma, in their own ways, and many others like Malala. She is one of the first women to do Hajj alone and to author a book like this on UK society.

Zahra does have her own identity.

What Religious Scholar?

Zahra and her big Sufi sister Rahma made sweet Pakistani rice a month ago. As Zahra has not been at home much, she does not know to make such things, so her sister showed her. Then this month, they kept the food simple, but Zahra went to help, and both sisters got talking.

Zahra and her sister talked about many things, but they also talked about their lives if they were in Pakistan and not the UK and how both sisters' lives had turned out.

When Rahma Zahra's Sufi sister said, "Zahra consult a religious scholar," Zahra asked her sister, "which scholar?" Because both have been bought up with Islam around, but their lives turned out so different. Her sister went silent.

Zahra once said to a brother who once asked how she "can follow a faith that gives women a lesser share of a parent's estate," Zahra said, "actually brother, now that I am read, it is not Islam or any faith that is wrong, it is people."

The brother, like Salman, said you are an intelligent woman. The brother does much work with people in Bollywood and Lollywood; he said, "you are an interesting woman, but very different."

In December 2022, this Serbian man said, "I am a Serbian man, I am a giant, and I cannot understand how I am sitting opposite this Pakistani woman, and I enjoy her company." Zahra tried to ignore what he really said; she said, "we are friends."

She told Rahma, she was not sure she approved of Zahra hanging out alone with a Serbian man.

Allah has made people better than all his creations, and he did that for a reason; Zahra thinks one should use their life and skills to do some good and is now interested in legacy work.

Rahma has a deep Muslim history; they are one of the UK's first Sufis; Zahra stays involved as the family reminds her of her parents, their parents, and her bachpan, which means childhood in Urdu.

People met at their house before for Sunday religious-focused gatherings; there were no local UK mosques then.

But Zahra agrees with Salman that we should go directly to Allah. Allah told the Prophet Muhammad through Jibrael (Gabriel); he said, "read," and we should read ourselves too. The Prophet could not read before. Nadeer says to Zahra, after all that reading, "you know a lot."

Zahra likes her old friends.

Free Books

The blue book Zahra made says, "diversity in the UK Construction Industry," and then, "Masters of Business Administration in Construction and Real Estate." This is the front cover of Zahra's dissertation from 2011; she likes the book's simplicity.

Zahra thinks she will get this book bound in green; Zahra likes green a lot, and the colour is like miti, which means earth, but we shall see.

To those named in the book, Zahra will send a free copy. Zahra will also send free copies to people to influence social change, with a note of her thoughts.

Zahra will write to the University of Oxford to see if there is some way in which we may one day attend a graduation ceremony, as she missed her sons.

She knows they do honorary degrees; some establishments offer honorary fellowships, Zahra's son used to say, "you deserve an award." She will also send a copy to Queen Mary's University and other similar establishments, such as secondary schools.

Zahra will offer the book to the market to help seed fund her community interest endeavour.

Then Zahra shall author other books to help society, particularly in deprived communities, and hold online sessions to help develop understanding. She will build her network of like-minded people and continue with APC coaching work.

In 2022 in the UK, a little 2-year-old boy called Awaab Ishak should not have died from dampness in his property. Seventy-two people should not have died in the Grenfell fire in 2017; the families said, "we told the authorities."

We live in a divided society, and Zahra likes the idea of little kids' books, as they can speak English and, in some homes, adults cannot.

If Zahra can help build bridges in society, she will do this; she was taught how to interpret very well at home from a little age.

Zahra has a lot to offer.

Chapter 7. Be Brave

The Grenfell Tower fire was a sombre day in UK history; it took place on 14 June 2017.

Zahra remembers it was Ramadan, and, in the night, she recalls driving past the tower after she read Taraweeh at Central London Mosque. As many Muslims had finished Taraweeh, local people spotted a problem and went around the Tower to wake people up.

People the next day cried, "Thank God for Ramadan," otherwise, more would have died. People in the UK then began to view Muslims differently, and many Muslim charities did some excellent work to help with the disaster, including the local Al-Manaar Centre.

There was a photo in Inside Housing in November 2022 and a magazine article.

The following pages show the all-white Executive; one says the tower was a "case study," maybe a test case, and the other that "we did not need to give them ale," that is to persuade them to pass the product. It is hard to read; to make money, people do many things; at Hajj, you see that too.

This can sadly be life.

Faith and Professional Practice.

People say Zahra is the first. They say she combines faith with practice, particularly in real estate and surveying.

While Zahra wrote, she thought often. Zahra has had some incredibly good moments. Zahra has also had some incredibly low moments too.

With time she has learned that patience is best. Patience means sabr in Arabic and Urdu as we see in Surah Kahf. That is the 18th chapter of the Quran. A loss or a delay is not always deprivation. It is Allah's divine plan to give better.

Zahra learned this from Hajj. Hajj is a Muslim pilgrimage. There are pilgrimages in other faiths. We are travellers in this life as we have a temporary life. We ought to work towards creating a good life.

Zahra likes Surah Imran, Quran Chapters 3-4. The description of Mary (Maryum), Quran 3:37. Hidden away, Allah provided for Maryum, Quran 3:37.

Also, Surah Maryum, Quran Chapter 19. It is true, "Your Lord never forgets" Quran 19:64. It is about Tawakkul, which is to trust God's plan. Zahra has learned to trust God's plan.

In 2022, if book writing is what He wants her to do, then OK. While she has no income, Allah will look after her for now.

Child of God

Zahra has decided it best to stay single. She thinks a relationship would be too restrictive. Zahra has not fought all her life to be free. To be put in a cage again. She likes to be free.

Insha'Allah (God willing) when she dies. She is sure some good person will find and bury her. Because in the end. That is our final home. And there is no point in being dead when you are still alive.

Zahra is grateful to her parents. Her ex-husband, too, and his family. Her sons as they gave her purpose. And friends. Also, her work.

Everyone says, "be free," and her sisters too.

When a person has Allah as a friend, they have their best friend; Allah is Wali, the protector, Quran 2:257.

Remember, the Prophet Muhammad had no one; his father died before he was born, his mother Aminah died when he was young, and he had no siblings. All the Prophet's children except Fatimah Zahra died before him; she died a few months after her father.

The Prophet Muhammad's wife, Khadijah, is a powerful example of a good businessperson. She worked from the back in Saudi Arabia when women traders were rare; in 2022, Zahra thinks there is a lot to be drawn from history; she learned a lot.

Khadijah also died before the Prophet Muhammad, as did his uncle Abu Talib.

We should learn to read and write and build our own spiritual connection; alone is an opportunity.

A Person in a Green Dress Takes a Selfie.

This is Zahra at Hajj; she did not know which hotel she would stay at, but Allah placed her in one of the best in Makkah.

While she was alone, Allah took care of her.

This was Zahra's photo from July 2022.

But Zahra took the photo away as Allah placed her there, it may as well be someone else, and one day, she will be dead.

Zahra hopes her story will live on for people to learn about 2022, Hajj, and other lessons they may draw on families, society, and work.

Zahra replaced her photo with one of a prayer mat Zahra bought from Madinah before returning to London, UK, from Hajj in Saudi Arabia.

It is a premium mat, like Zahra's books. The mats are the same as what you find at the Prophet's Mosque in Madinah.

Zahra will sell her books as special because Allah has given women a special status in Islam; it came to free the oppressed, both women, men, and enslaved people.

In the old days, girls would be buried as little children; if you had no tribe or master, you were nothing.

A brown divorced woman with two little children, now no children and no father or mother, or family or local community, would be nothing too.

That is the same person in the green dress.

This is the person's end; Zahra has seen many deaths, and it reminds one of their mortality.

In the end, everything will be left behind, and one should adopt a traveller mindset.

Advice to Your 50-year-old self.

Focus on yourself, as no one is going to look after you. You cannot do anything about what has passed, but you can learn from it to make things better in the future and make your own life right. So, Zahra has an action plan for 2023.

But let us see …

The Ending

And ...

May God (Allah) give us good in this life and good in our afterlife.

Amen (Ameen)

Charity

Please forgive any errors; as Zahra said at the start, she is not a religious scholar, but this is Zahra's form of charity; today and in the future, some lessons can be drawn from her story and others' lives, particularly from old people.

Zahra is sorry she did not get to know her parents more, but as Rahma said, "they did not talk too."

Influences

Shaykh Yasir Qadhi's YouTube videos on the Seerah and the life of the Prophet Muhammad are detailed and exciting; Zahra listened to sixty-three of the 103 one-hour lectures. He has many degrees and accolades.

Zahra listened to Shaykh's final lectures on the Prophet's life to learn how the Prophet died; she cried a lot and learned to love the Prophet through the lessons.

The Majestic Quran by Musharraf Hussain; after her elder Sufi sister posted one of the thinking points, it triggered her interest and was easy to read.

The Al-Quran Al-Karim, Othmani Rasm in English. The Noble Quran, word-by-word translation, and colour-coded Tajweed. She likes this version as under the Arabic text is the English meaning.

Omar Suleiman's 30 for thirty series in Ramadan 2020.

Yasmin Mogahed, "Reclaim your Heart."

Waleed Basyouni of Al Maghreb in the US. Shamsiya Noorul Quloob, the Ideal Muslimah. Safi Kaskas. Also, various others on Facebook.

Nouman Ali Khan; a few years ago, Zahra began to listen to him on YouTube; when he came to London, she attended one of his lectures; it was on Noor and the light inside everyone.

Omid Safi, a Professor of Islamic Studies at Duke University in the US. Waleed Basyouni of the Al Maghrib Institute.

Justin Elias posts on Instagram; it says he is the Author of Daily Hadith Online, focusing on primary text and information on the Prophet Muhammad.

Abdal Hakim Murad, born Timothy John Winter, Zahra liked his lectures on Seclusion and Love; they were apt during the Covid pandemic.

The YMCA and its founder, George Williams, was born in Somerset, England. Like Zahra, he was born on 11 October 1821. In 1844 he joined eleven friends and organized the first Young Men's Christian Association, a refuge of Bible study and prayer for young men seeking escape.

Zahra likes what they say about Jesus (Isa in Islam)'s approach to service, in that he considers it a great honour to serve people.

Zahra also mentioned the Son of David, she does not know if he were telling the truth, but he left a mark on her, he was an Orthodox Jewish man, and Zahra could see that was how he was bought up.

Like Zahra, he also said, "he is not a religious person," because Zahra is not. She knows that her current thoughts can change, and she may not be interested in religion in the future.

Zahra has learned a lot from self-study, she navigates text from all the places, and the MBA taught her the discipline to look for the source.

Sometimes, when she posts on LinkedIn and has not checked the source, some brothers will message her privately to say, "sister, that may not be right."

Glossary of Terms

Bachpan, which means childhood. Miti, which means earth in Urdu.

Dhu al-Hijrah is the last month in the Islamic calendar.

Fajr, morning salah, prayers at sunrise. The other three prayers are called Zuhr afternoon prayers. Asr and late afternoon prayer. Isha evening prayer. Maghreb, evening salah, prayers at sunset.

Hafiz is someone that has memorised the Quran.

Hajjan is a title for a woman after she has performed Hajj. Haji a title for a man after he has performed Hajj.

Hajj is the fifth pillar of Islam; it means to make a journey.

Ihram is simple clothing, two white sheets for men and modest Islamic women's clothing.

Infaq is an Arabic word to mean spending and disbursement, but it also carries the sense of doing so to please Allah without asking for any favour or hoping for a return.

Insha'Allah it means God willing.

Motawif is an online platform the Saudi Arabian Government used for pilgrims to book Hajj in 2022.

Qurbani is a ritual animal sacrifice.

Sabr means patience.

Salah is the five daily prayers, the second pillar of Islam.

Sawn, which is too fast in the month of Ramadan, is the fourth pillar of Islam.

Seerah is a person's journey through life.

Shahadah is the declaration of faith, the first pillar of Islam.

Sufi, Sufism is about the Islamic faith and combining it with practice.

Taraweeh is a special prayer that involves an extended reading of the Quran.

Tawakkul is to trust God's plan.

Umrah is the little pilgrimage.

Wali. A protector.

Zakat, which is a charity, is the third pillar of Islam.

Zamzam water and holy water form a well in Makkah.

Glossary of Key Places

Al-Aqsa Mosque, next to the Dome of the Rock, is in Israel, Palestine. It is Islam's third most important mosque.

Arafah, The Mount of Arafah is the place where the Prophet Muhammad delivered the last sermon. It is known as the "Mountain of Mercy." Arafah is in Saudi Arabia, near Makkah. Pilgrims stay here during Hajj; it is a campsite.

Jamarat is symbolic of when Prophet Ibrahim fought the devil but threw three stones at him. Pilgrims visit here also.

Kaabah, which Muslims believe to be the house of God.

Masjid Al-Haram, Makkah, Saudi Arabia; is Islam's most important mosque. It is the direction of prayer for Muslims worldwide.

Masjid E-Nabwi, Madinah, Saudi Arabia, is the second most important mosque.

Mina is in Saudi Arabia, again near Makkah. Mina means to be put to the test. Muslims believe that Mina is connected to the test Allah put Prophet Ibrahim when she was told to sacrifice his son. Mina is the place where he was tested. Pilgrims stay here during Hajj; it is a campsite.

Muzdalifah. To stay one night under the Muzdalifah open sky represents equality and seeking repentance from Allah. Pilgrims stay here during Hajj; it is a campsite.

Rawdah is a place in Madinah and Masjid E-Nabwi where the Prophet Muhammad is buried.

Safa and Marwah. Muslims believe a spring formed when Prophet Ismail kicked the floor as a baby as he was thirty, while his mother Hajar, wife of Prophet Ibrahim, ran between the Mountains of Safa and Marwah in Makkah.

The Al-Manaar Centre, near West London, UK.

The Central London Mosque, Regents Park, in the UK.

The West London Islamic Centre, in West London, UK.

Glossary of Organisations

Al-Manaar

ASRA

Arab News

Cabinet Office

Central London Mosque

College of Estate Management

Dome Tours, a UK tour operator

Fisabilillah Publications

Fulham Cross

Hammersmith and West London College

Home Group

Imran Khan Cancer Hospital

Inside Housing

LB Brent

Local Government Association

Malala Yousufzai

Miles Coverdale

Muslim Council of Britain.

one YMCA

Queen Mary's University

Shepherds Bush Mosque

Southern Housing Group

Thames Valley University

The Association of Project Managers

The Chartered Institute of Building

The Institute of Housing

The Institute of Management

The Royal Institution of Chartered Surveyors

The University of Reading University

The University of Oxford.

The University of Cambridge.

University College of Estate Management

West London Islamic Centre, West Ealing, London

William Sutton Housing Trust

Printed in Great Britain
by Amazon

18545186R00058